CALPURNIA TATE 🔔 GIRL VET

GOATS FOR CHRISTMAS

BY **JACQUELINE KELLY**

WITH ILLUSTRATIONS BY JENNIFER L. MEYER

GODWINBOOKS

HENRY HOLT AND COMPANY · NEW YORK

For animal lovers everywhere

Henry Holt and Company, *Publishers since 1866*
Henry Holt® is a registered trademark of Macmillan Publishing Group, LLC
120 Broadway, New York, NY 10271 · mackids.com

Our books may be purchased in bulk for promotional, educational, or business use. Please
contact your local bookseller or the Macmillan Corporate and Premium Sales Department
at (800) 221-7945 ext. 5442 or by email at MacmillanSpecialMarkets@macmillan.com.

Library of Congress Control Number: 2021906600

First edition, 2021
Designed by Trisha Previte
Printed in the United States of America by
LSC Communications, Crawfordsville, Indiana

ISBN 978-1-62779-879-2

1 3 5 7 9 10 8 6 4 2

The main trouble with goats is that they'll eat just about anything. Did you know that? There are lots of other troubles with goats, but that's the main one—and the one that got my brother Travis into trouble at Christmas.

Travis, if you remember, is the soft-hearted brother who is crazy about animals, so crazy that he's never met an animal he doesn't want to lug home right away. Even when the poor struggling animal *wants no part of this plan.* Believe me, there are plenty of wild animals out there that don't appreciate being scooped up and dragged home by an eleven-year-old boy. Sometimes our barn looks like a regular zoo. Sometimes he tries to smuggle the unhappy creatures into his bedroom, and Mother just about has a fit when she finds out. (It's a good thing we live in Texas instead of Africa—we'd have monkeys swinging from the curtains, and lion cubs under the bed, and pink flamingos in the sink. It would all be a dreadful mess; trust me. But let's get back to goats.)

Our little town of Fentress has a Christmas pageant every year with a Nativity scene. The local men build a sort of shed, and our neighbors dress in costumes as Joseph and Mary and the angels and the three wise men and the shepherds. Over the years, my six brothers have played different parts, and this year it was Travis's turn to play one of the shepherds. My older brother Lamar—a real pill—was playing one of the wise men. That was a joke if ever I'd heard one. I hadn't been asked to play anything, which was fine by me. It's usually pretty cold, and you have to

stand there for a couple of hours, so they use a rubber doll to play the part of baby Jesus. There are usually a few sheep and a cow and a horse and some-times a donkey. Travis and I always hope for a camel, but we have no idea where to find one.

When I don't know what to do about something, I go to Granddaddy. He knows everything about everything. I found him in the library surrounded by his vast collection of books and bones, feathers and fossils, dried plants and bottled beasts.

"Granddaddy," I said, "we need a

camel. Where can I find one?"

"An interesting question," he said, looking up from his reading. "Do you need a one-humped camel from Africa or a two-humped camel from Asia?"

"I think either would do, really. Is it true their humps are full of water?"

"A common misconception. The humps are actually full of stored fat so the beasts can go for many days without food. But as you can see, I do not have a single member of the Camelidae family in my collection. Why do you require one?"

"We need a camel for the Christmas manger scene."

"Ah. Well, since you ask, there were actually camels in Texas before the War." By this he meant the War Between the States.

"*Really?*" I'd had no idea. Maybe we'd run into a camel on one of our many Nature Rambles.

"The army imported dozens of the beasts fifty years ago to haul supplies between military posts across the Southwest. In fact, they were settled near Kerrville, not that far from here."

"Gosh," I said. "Are they still alive?"

"There may be a few left wandering about in far-west Texas, but it's unlikely."

7

"What happened to them?"

"They worked well in the desert, thrifty beasts and hardy. But they spooked the horses and the mules, and their drivers found them to be bad-tempered and evil-smelling. It's a shame. They were eventually sold off or turned loose in the wild to fend for themselves."

"That's all very interesting, but I guess it means no camel for us."

"Sadly not. Now if you'll excuse me, I must finish my study of the blind salamander recently discovered in the San Marcos Springs."

"Wait, it's truly blind?"

"Indeed. After living for millions of years in total darkness, it has slowly lost the use of its eyes."

I pondered this. "What does it live on? How does it hunt?"

"Fittingly, it lives on tiny shrimp that are also blind. It hunts them by sensing the vibrations of their movement in the water."

Blind salamanders chasing blind shrimp. Imagine swimming after your dinner in pitch darkness. The world is full of marvelous things.

I kissed him on the cheek and ran out to the barn, where I found Travis holding Bunny, his enormous fluffy white rabbit. They were something to behold: Bunny's fur had grown thick for winter, and he overflowed Travis's arms—a huge rabbit cuddled by a small boy.

"Any luck with a camel?" he said.

"No, but there actually used to be army camels in Texas." I told him what I'd learned.

"But that doesn't help us," he said.

"That's true."

He thought for a moment and said,

"I have an idea. I think we can make a camel."

"Travis Tate," I said, "you've lost your mind. What on earth are you talking about?"

He pointed at King Arthur, one of our big plow horses, dozing calmly in his stall. "We could make some kind of hump and stick it on Arthur. He's about the right size, don't you think?"

"Yes, but . . ."

"Do you have a better idea?" Travis said.

"No, but . . ."

Since I couldn't come up with anything better, we spent all afternoon making a "hump" for Arthur, which turned out to be a much bigger job than we'd expected. First, we had to find a bunch of burlap sacks, and then we had to rip them apart, and then we had to find a bunch of twine. Then we sewed the sacks together in a sort of hump-like shape, stuffed it with hay, and hoisted it over Arthur's back. He barely even noticed.

We stepped back to admire our work. And you know what? Arthur looked exactly like a plow horse with a huge, misshapen bag of hay plopped on his back. We stood in silence for a long time. Finally, I said, "You know, Travis, he doesn't really—"

"I know," he said, looking very glum. "You don't have to say it."

"Cheer up," I said. "It was a good idea. Or at least it was an idea, and it *was* the only one we had, and you *do* have to work with what you've got. And not every Christmas scene has to have a camel. We'll still have a cow and a horse and some sheep, and you're playing the shepherd, so that will be fine."

But I turned out to be wrong about that. There was an unexpected shortage of sheep in our town that month. There were, however, plenty of goats.

One of our neighbors, Mr. Morgan, had bought a new herd of goats and had a bunch of extra kids running around (the goat kind, not the human kind). He was willing to lend them to the cause of the pageant.

Our shepherd complained some about that. "The Bible says that *shepherds* watched over their flock by night," Travis said. "That means sheep, not goats. I'm going to look kind of silly watching goats."

"You're going to look sillier watching nothing at all," I said. "Come on, let's get some goats."

We found a couple of old collars and some rope and went to Mr. Morgan's. He took us to a field where a dozen kids milled around, *maa*-ing and nudging us for food. Their cries sounded much like a human baby calling for its mother. They were of many colors and patterns with splotches of white and black and rusty brown all over them, and were really very cute, with alert faces and floppy ears and upright tails. Their pupils were rectangular rather than round, which made them look full of mischief and, well, a little eerie.

"Which ones do you want?" Mr. Morgan said. "It makes no never mind to me." A handsome brown-and-white male nibbled on Travis's bootlaces.

"Sir, what's this one's name?" said Travis.

"Name? Son, they don't have names. That one there is Number Seven."

Travis patted the goat and scratched behind his ears. Number Seven seemed to like this and gently butted my brother's leg. I noticed the goat had horns. Not very big ones, true, but still, they counted as horns.

"Okay," said Travis, "we'll take this one. And how about that female over there? The one that looks like she's wearing a hat."

Mr. Morgan waded into the herd

and brought us another kid. She was all white except for a patch of black over her forehead and one eye. It did indeed look as if she was wearing a hat tilted at a rakish angle.

"This here is Number Eleven," said Mr. Morgan. "Is that enough, or do you want some more?"

"How many can we have?" said Travis. If left to his own devices, he'd have taken the whole bunch home.

"Two will be fine," I said quickly.

"But I'm supposed to be watching a flock," said Travis.

"Two is definitely a flock," I said, "or at least pretty close."

"A flock means a bunch," he said. "Two is not a bunch."

"Two is *plenty*, Travis."

Mr. Morgan said, "Son, maybe you should listen to your sister. These goats are a handful. Now, you feed them good and bring them back to me in good shape, all right?"

"We will, Mr. Morgan."

We slipped the collars over their heads and, oh, how they hated that. They panicked and jumped and

thrashed like hooked fish. This was clearly not going to work.

"Here you go," said Mr. Morgan, slipping their collars off and lifting them into our arms. "They're not used to wearing a collar. It's easier if you just carry them home. You can do that, right?"

We could. Barely. Twenty minutes later, we staggered into our barn and put the goats in a small pen. They looked at us with curiosity. Number Seven nuzzled Travis.

Travis caught his breath and said,

"You know, Callie, they are awful cute."

Uh-oh. I knew what was coming.

"When this is all over, I wonder if we could—"

"Absolutely not."

"But you don't know what I was going to say."

"I do know what you were going to say. I absolutely do."

Number Seven licked Travis's hand, which did not help the situation. Travis stared at him thoughtfully. "At least I could give him a proper name, don't you think?"

"No, I don't."

"Everybody needs a name. You can't go through life without a name."

"You absolutely can. Do you name the birds flying overhead? No, you do not. Do you name the bees buzzing in the hive? No, you do not."

"This is different. How'd you like to be called by a number?"

"If I were a goat, I'm pretty sure I wouldn't care, and neither would you."

"It just doesn't seem right." He studied the male. "I'm going to call this one . . . Buster." Buster *maa*-ed in what sounded like approval.

"Travis, really?"

"And I'm going to call the one with the hat . . . let's see . . . Hattie."

There was no stopping the boy. I sighed heavily, something I do a lot when it comes to Travis and animals. Buster and Hattie looked hungry, so we fed them each a handful of oats, which they inhaled, sniffing around for the last little flake. Then I heard Mother calling me from the back porch.

"Calpurnia," she cried, "it's time for your practice!"

"Drat." The piano in the parlor awaited me for the next half hour. "Travis, look, you have to get them used

to the collars. You work on that while I'm gone, okay?"

"Okay."

I ran inside and did battle with the piano while Mother darned socks and mended shirts on the sofa behind me. Although I couldn't see her, I swear I could feel her wince every time I hit a sour note. I watched the clock and sprang to my feet a half hour later, to the relief of all.

"Well," I said, "that's it for today. I'll be out in the barn. We have to get the shepherd and his flock ready."

"It's odd," Mother said. "You practice

the piano every day, and you have a lesson every week, but you never seem to improve very much. I don't understand it."

"Me neither," I said, which was a lie. The reason I never improved is that my heart wasn't in it. I just didn't care. I'd much rather have spent my time with Granddaddy on Nature Rambles, or rowing with him down the river, or digging up fossils and arrowheads together. But I knew this wouldn't sit well with Mother.

Trying hard not to sound too eager, I said, "Maybe I could give up the piano?"

She frowned. "Certainly not. Perhaps

if you applied yourself more." Playing the piano was part of her goal of making a proper young lady of me. Fat chance of that. Then she said these terrible words: "We may have to double your practice time in order to see some progress." A cold shudder ran through me. (And guess what? After that, it turned out my playing got quite a bit better. Funny how that happens.)

I ran back to the barn and found Travis brushing each collarless goat in turn. They looked very happy.

"What are you doing? I said. "Put those collars on right now."

"They don't like it."

"Too bad."

We cornered them in the small pen and wrestled the collars onto them. Once again they acted like we were torturing them.

"Quick," I said, "more oats." And it worked—it turns out that all it took to calm them down was another handful of oats. And another. And another.

"Keep them distracted with food," I said.

"They sure do eat a lot," Travis said.

"Well, they're growing kids."

They *did* eat a lot, and not just food.

They nibbled on our hands, and Travis's sleeve, and my pinafore. At one point I made the mistake of turning my back on them to check their water trough.

"Uh, Callie?" said Travis.

"What?"

"Hattie's eating your braid."

29

"*What?*" I whipped around and was pulled up short—the end of my braid was halfway down Hattie's gullet. I tugged on it and she tugged back.

"Don't just stand there," I yelled at Travis. "*Help me!*"

Together we managed to retrieve my hair, now covered with goat slime. But my ribbon was gone for good.

"Yuck," I said.

We turned in time to see Buster swallowing a piece of sack.

"Oh no," Travis said, "they'll get sick. Should we take them to the vet? Mr. Morgan's going to be so mad."

"No need to worry," I said. "I've heard that goats have cast-iron stomachs."

But just in case, we sat watch over them for the rest of the afternoon. They were fine. In fact, they were so

perfectly fine that they kept snuf-
fling around for the next thing to eat.
We took off their collars and moved
them to the outside pen with the huge
live oak.

The next day I sat with Travis in his room while he tried on his "robes." Mother had made them from old sheets she'd stitched together, with one over his head secured by a belt.

"You look like a real shepherd," I said, "except where's your crook?"

"I don't have one. Will that be okay?"

"We'll find you a big stick; that'll do. Let's go out and show the goats your costume." When we got to the outside pen, there were no goats to be seen.

"Oh no." Had they been eaten by coyotes in the night? But there was no blood on the ground and no sign of a struggle. So they'd escaped. Or been stolen. Which meant we'd have to pay Mr. Morgan back.

"Callie," Travis said.

How much did two goats cost? How long would it take to pay for them? Months, no doubt.

"Hey, Callie."

I tried to remember how much money I had saved up in the tin box under my bed. Did Travis have any money saved, or had he spent his allowance on his pets as he usually did?

"Hey, Callie, look."

Could we throw ourselves on the mercy of Mother and Father to pay for them?

"Look up there," he said, pointing to the top of the tall oak.

And there, on the very highest of the very high limbs, stood Buster and Hattie, daintily cropping the leaves.

"Yikes!"

"So how do we get them down?" said Travis.

I thought fast. "Well, since they got themselves up there, I figure they can probably get themselves down. Go and get some oats."

I studied the goats while Travis ran to the barn. They looked very much at home, scampering along slender limbs that bowed alarmingly under their

weight, hopping from branch to branch, as agile as cats. Who knew that goats could climb trees?

Travis came back with a can of oats.

"Come down from there," I yelled. They ignored me. I rattled the can of oats and that caught their attention, sure enough. I rattled it again and—as quick as a flash—they practically ran down the tree headfirst and landed safely beside us, pushing each other aside to get at the food.

"Wow," said Travis. "I didn't know they could do that. Did you?"

"Uh . . . yeah, of course."

Buster and Hattie followed us, along with the rattling can of oats, all the way back to the barn.

"Travis," I said, "it's only four days until the pageant. You have to get them used to the collars."

"I will. I promise."

Hmm.

Rattle
Rattle

3

The next day we woke up to the wonderful smell of gingerbread drifting through the house. Since there was no one to tell me not to, I slid down the banister to get to the kitchen as fast as I could. Our cook, Viola, was busy hauling a tray of gingerbread men out of the oven. I counted them over her shoulder: seven.

"One each for you and the boys," she said. "I'm going to set them over here, and don't you touch 'em. Got that?"

"Yes, Viola." In the kitchen, her word was the law.

"You can ice 'em if you want after they cool. But let 'em cool real good first. You got that?"

"Yes, ma'am."

I had iced last year's cookies before they'd cooled all the way. The icing had melted and puddled and run all over the place, and they looked pretty terrible. That pill Lamar laughed at me for days. In my defense, I have to agree that although they didn't look so good, they tasted just fine.

While waiting for the cookies to cool, I sought out Granddaddy in the library. "Granddaddy," I said, "do you know what I want to talk about today?"

"No, but I suspect you will tell me."

"Goats," I said.

"Indeed? And why is that?"

"It's the Christmas pageant. We couldn't get a camel, and we couldn't get any sheep, so we ended up with goats."

"I see. Well, they are related to both sheep and antelope. Their stomachs are composed of four chambers, and they chew the cud. Their horns are made of keratin, the same material as hair and fingernails. They are intelligent and curious, as I'm sure you've noticed."

"Yes, and yesterday they climbed to the top of a tree. How can they do that with hooves? Why is their balance so good?"

Granddaddy pulled one of his books from a shelf and opened it to a picture of a shaggy goat standing on the side of what looked like a sheer cliff.

"See here," he said, "your goats are descended from these wild mountain goats of Asia Minor. As a survival mechanism, they evolved the ability to cling to steep rock ledges on the mountainside where predators could not follow. Their hooves have two toes that

can spread apart to afford secure foot-
ing. They also developed the ability to
live on very tough vegetation, which is
why they can eat so many things. But I
leave the rest of the research to you."

"Thank you." I pulled my Scientific
Notebook from my pinafore pocket and
made careful note of these facts.

"Now," he said, "I'm going for a
walk. Would you care to accompany
me?"

"Yes, please." I loved going on these
Nature Rambles. I ran upstairs for the
fishing creel he'd given me and my
butterfly net. The creel was the perfect

size for holding my notebook and specimen jars. And even though it wasn't butterfly season, the net was handy for catching other things as well. I ran back down and rejoined him on the front porch, grateful that I hadn't been spotted by Mother or Viola. The cookies could wait. Besides, they weren't going to cool any faster with me hanging about and staring at them.

"Where are we going today?" I said. "I thought upstream for a change."

We walked to the river and turned upstream. A crow cawed as we pushed our way through the brush.

"Ah," said Granddaddy, "the sentry has spotted us and is warning the others."

"They have a sentry? Like in the army?"

"Indeed. Crows are members of the Corvidae family, which includes ravens and blue jays. They are intelligent birds, playful and social, and they have a family structure similar to that of human families. They can also learn to talk."

"We better not tell Travis. He'll want one."

"Which one is Travis again?"

46

"He's the younger one that keeps adopting wild animals."

"Ah yes, that one. That boy is misguided in his attempts to domesticate wildlife. Still, he could do worse than a crow."

"Let's not tell him that," I said.

"Agreed."

The crow cawed again. From across the inlet came an answering cry. We kept walking, and a couple of crows followed us all the way to the third bend in the river.

Granddaddy had taught me to look closely, to listen closely, to observe all

47

things in Nature closely. I couldn't see
the crows very well, so I listened hard
to their calls back and forth. At first
they sounded exactly the same. But
after a minute I could hear a slight dif-
ference in their voices. They did seem
to be talking to one another, perhaps
discussing our progress along the river.
I imagined them saying, "Here comes
that girl and her grandfather again.
They're always poking around
down there—who knows

why?—but they seem harmless enough."

Much of the wildlife had disappeared for the winter. The flying creatures had flown south for warmer parts; the burrowing creatures had disappeared underground; the climbing creatures had hidden themselves away in hollow trees. But still, if you knew *how* to look, and *where* to look, what seemed like a bare landscape actually teemed with life. I managed to scoop up some dragonfly nymphs with my net and put them in a jar of water for later study.

After an hour we cut across Dawson's farm to walk home on the road. We ran into Dr. Pritzker returning from a farm call in his wagon. Dr. Pritzker is the town's animal doctor. (The fancy word for this is *veterinarian*.) One of his hands was clawed up from an old rattlesnake bite, so sometimes he let me help him prepare his pills and powders

and make labels for the bottles. Sometimes, if I was really lucky, he'd let me go with him when he doctored sick animals. And sometimes, if I was really *really* lucky, Mother didn't find out about it.

He reined his mare, Penny, to a halt and said, "Would you like a lift home?"

"Thank you kindly," Granddaddy said. "Shall we ride or walk, Calpurnia?"

"Let's ride," I said, and we climbed aboard.

If it had been a farm wagon, I would have voted to keep walking, but

Granddaddy and Dr. Pritzker always found interesting things to talk about, and I always found it interesting to listen in. Today the talk was of the latest dinosaur fossils in Colorado. I learned that Professor Cope and Professor Marsh were digging up startling fossils at a great rate. The two men were competitors and hated each other's guts. They spied on each other's camps and stole bones from each other's digs. All this was very interesting, but it seemed a shame; they would have made much better progress if they'd been able to work together. The latest find was a forty-foot tall flesh-eater with rows of teeth like daggers, a real nightmare if ever there was one. Good thing they didn't exist anymore, or Travis would have found a baby one and dragged it home. Hmm, now that was something to think about. No doubt they'd win the blue ribbon at the Fall Fair pet show, since people usually brought things like cats and dogs.

One year Dovie Medlin, this really boring girl, brought her goldfish Bubbles in a bowl. I mean, really, when you compare a goldfish with a dinosaur? There's no contest.

4

$\mathcal{B}$ack at the house, everyone was in a frenzy of preparation with non-stop cooking and cleaning. The house—and everyone in it—had to be spotless for the holidays. I was put to work in the kitchen stirring and pouring and measuring. I iced the gingerbread men

and the three-layered chocolate wal-
nut cake, a tricky job but extremely
worthwhile in that I got to lick the beat-
ers afterward and I didn't have to fight

my brothers for them. Clouds of steam and the wonderful smells of spiced apples and cloves and oranges drifted out of the kitchen, and yet for all the hard work, everyone remained in good spirits.

Finally I was able to sneak away to the general store and buy presents for my brothers, little brown paper bags filled with penny candy: caramel clusters and glossy licorice and chewy jujubes, peanut brittle and chocolate

squares, marshmallow puffs and jelly beans in all different colors.

When I came out of the store, I ran into Milly Thompson sitting on the steps, cradling one of her many little sisters. Milly came from a poor family at the far end of town. She and the baby were both dressed in old hand-me-down clothes, and looked cold and pinched and ragged. I'd once given her some of my old books since she had none of her own. Can you imagine not having any books? It was beyond me. She'd thought I'd hung the moon ever since.

"Hi, Callie. Merry Christmas to you." She smiled shyly.

"Hi, Milly. I hope you have a merry Christmas too."

She caught sight of the bags of candy and blinked, the oddest look on her face. Oh. It was the look of someone who never got candy.

I still had a nickel in my pocket. I'd planned to put it back in the tin box of my savings, where it would sit in the dark, shoved under the far corner of my bed. Or I could do something else with it. Was it not better to pluck that nickel from the dark? Was it not better to take this little metal disc and turn it into a little brown paper bag of joy for someone with very little joy in her life?

"Stay there, Milly. I'll be right back." I turned and went back into the store, the bell tinkling merrily overhead. I took my time and chose carefully, then went outside and handed her the bag.

"Here you go, Milly; this is for you. Merry Christmas." The look on her face was worth a hundred nickels.

I skipped back home, filled with the Christmas spirit. Then it was time to fetch the Christmas tree. My oldest brother, Harry, hitched Arthur to the

wagon, and my brothers and I piled in to pick a tree from a neighbor who had a large stand of junipers on his property. You probably think this sounds like a lot of fun, right? Not so. There were always squabbles. Between the seven of us children, we held seven different opinions about which tree was exactly the right tree.

"*This* one," said Lamar, bossy as always.

"Why that one?" I said.

"Because it's the best one."

"It is not," I said. "Look at the other side; it's practically bald."

"Oh, and your pick is better?"

"My pick is *much* better."

Harry sighed. "This happens every year and I'm tired of it. Why can't we all agree for once?"

I thought about this and said, "Harry's right. It's not very Christmassy of us. You decide, Harry. That'll be easiest."

To keep the peace, Harry wisely ignored my tree and Lamar's tree and found a tree of his own choosing. He chopped it down with a hatchet, and we drove back home singing carols. The only things missing were snow and an

open sleigh to dash through it.

We got the tree inside the parlor and decorated it with paper stars and strands of popcorn and something new called tinsel, long silver strips that glittered in the firelight. Father placed a tinfoil star on the very top, and we stood back to admire our work.

Father said, "Let's have a song." He led us in "We Three Kings":

Star of wonder, star of night,
Star with royal beauty bright.
Westward leading, still proceeding,
Guide us to thy perfect light.

Mother smiled at this rare moment of peace between her children. Which was wrecked five minutes later when Lamar sneaked up behind me and yanked on my braid for no good reason. Between goats and brothers, I could barely call my hair my own. I turned to slap him, but he ducked out of the way.

Mother rubbed her temples and said, "You two stop bickering; you're giving me a headache. Why can't you get along for once? All I want for Christmas is for everyone to get along."

RING RING RING RING

I could see she didn't feel well. I thought how it must feel to be a mother hen watching two of her chicks peck at each other all the time. *All the time.* No wonder she got sick headaches. And suddenly I knew what my present to her would be: I vowed I would get along with Lamar, at least for the holidays. I would ignore his pillish behavior. I would be a good sister to him, even if he stayed a bad brother to me.

"Mother," I said, as nice as pie, "I'm sorry. I promise to get along with Lamar for all of Christmas. You'll see."

"Huh?" said Lamar. "What are you

talking about? Is this some kind of trick?"

"No, it's not a trick. We'll call a truce. It will be our Christmas present to Mother. Don't you think that's a good idea?"

Mother smiled through her pain. "That would be lovely, Calpurnia." She turned to my brother. "What do you say, Lamar?"

I could see him thinking like mad, looking for some kind of trick or trap. But there was none, unless you counted the trick of kindness or the trap of peace.

"Will you do that, Lamar?" said Mother. "For me?"

What could he say? He had to say yes; of course he did. He scuffed his boot in the carpet.

"Okay," he said, and he even sounded like he halfway meant it.

We had been at each other's throats for so long that at first I couldn't think of any way to be nice to him. But finally I came up with something. Harry played the piano, and as we sang carols, I realized that of all of us, Lamar sounded the best. Funny, I'd never noticed this before.

"You sound really good," I told him. "You're the best singer in the family."

He didn't say anything or even smile. But at least he didn't scowl, so that was some progress. Finally he nodded a grudging thanks. And you know what? That simple nod made me feel pretty good.

After supper I offered him the leftover half of my gingerbread man.

"Here you go," I said. I smiled at him and I meant it. His eyes grew big. "What's wrong with it?" he said.

"There's nothing wrong with it."

He inspected it closely. "Did you

drop it on the floor? Did the dog lick it? Did you spit on it?"

"Eww, no. There's nothing wrong with it, Lamar. I'm just trying to be nice. I thought I'd share it with you, that's all. I know how much you like gingerbread."

He still looked suspicious. Finally he said, "Uh . . . thanks . . . I guess."

"You're welcome." The oddest thing happened right then: I felt all warm inside.

The rest of the day he softened on the outside, but I could tell a part of him was still a bit sour on the inside. It really was too bad, but I didn't mind. If he couldn't bring himself to be nice to me, I was determined to be nice to him. I would turn the other cheek, even if it killed me. And if he got unbearable, well, I had a whole bunch of other brothers to choose from.

All the next day I was the kindest sister in the world. We stopped exchanging nasty faces when no one was looking. No pinching, no punching, no pranks. I put no frogs in his bed; he put no spiders on my pillow. It was odd, but he grew quieter and quieter. It seemed like keeping the mean part of him bottled up inside made him almost . . . sad.

Peace reigned. For two whole days.

Then I guess he couldn't stand it anymore; he had to let it out somehow. And since he couldn't pick on me, he picked on Travis instead. A big mistake. And he did it right in front of me, an even *bigger* mistake. Travis was coming down the steps at the back door when Lamar did one of his favorite mean things: He stuck out his foot and tripped him.

"Hey!" Travis yelled, windmilling his arms like crazy. He managed to stay on his feet and he wasn't hurt. But what really did it for me was Lamar's laugh, that terrible snicker that always made me want to punch him in the nose. But I couldn't punch him in the nose. I had to turn the other cheek. So I did. Which in this case meant not punching him in the nose but merely shoving him. As hard as I could. He tumbled onto the grass.

"Ow!" He jumped up, glaring at me and rubbing his funny bone.

I squinched up my face really tight and waved my fist in his face. "Don't you do that, Lamar. Don't you do that, 'cos next time I'll punch you in the nose, I swear."

Travis said meekly, "It's okay, Callie. He didn't hurt me."

"No, Travis, it's not okay. He's being a pill."

Lamar gave me the evil eye and dashed into the house. That was the end of our truce. After lunch he pinched me, so of course I had to stomp on his foot; there was nothing else for it.

Mother got one of her headaches.

Afew hours later I noticed that Travis had been keeping to himself. I finally cornered him.

"Travis, I've barely seen you today. What's going on?"

"Nothing, Callie. We've all been awful busy."

"Huh. So I guess you've been putting the collars on the goats, right? Getting them used to it, right?"

"Uh . . . yeah . . . a little . . . some."

"Travis."

"It's just that they hate it so much when I do it."

"Travis."

"Okay, okay, okay. You don't have to get all prickly about it."

"Really? It seems like I do. Come on, we're going to the barn right now." We slipped out the back door before anyone could trap us into more chores.

The goats were nestled in the straw

but leaped to their feet, *maaing* in excitement when they saw Travis. Buster and Hattie were sleek and well-brushed, and they looked good. Obviously Travis had been looking after them. There was only one thing missing—no, two things.

"Where are their collars?" I said.

He pulled them off a nail and handed them to me.

The goats saw them in my hand and huddled at the back of the pen.

"Get in here, Travis, help me."

Well, it was still a disaster. The goats bucked and kicked and butted and screamed bloody murder, sending all the other animals into a panic. Travis and I collapsed in the straw, panting and sweaty.

"What are we going to do?" Travis said, almost in tears.

"Don't get upset," I said. "I'll talk to Dr. Pritzker. If he can't help us, nobody can."

I caught my breath for a minute and then ran down the road to Dr. Pritzker's office. I found him hitching up Penny to go out on a call.

"Good day, Calpurnia."

"Good day, Dr. Pritzker. I have a problem."

"I thought you might; you have that look about you."

"I do?" This puzzled me. "What kind of look is that?"

"That look of pondering a problem. You wear it often."

"Oh. I didn't know anyone could tell."

"So what can I help you with?"

"It's goats," I said. "You look after goats, right?"

"Yes, but not often. They're tough little creatures, and they don't usually need my help." I explained our goaty problem. "We have to get them to calm down with their collars, and Travis isn't doing a very good job. They have to stay still while people come by and admire the scene."

"You need some goat-calming medicine?"

"Is there such a thing? If there is such a thing, I definitely need it."

"Not that I'm specifically aware of, but perhaps I can concoct something. Come back tomorrow morning and I'll think on it."

I sat at breakfast the next morning with Mother and Father and Granddaddy and my six brothers. Viola served up towers of flapjacks and mountains of fried eggs and whole loaves of toasted bread and crocks of sunny yellow butter from our own cow, Flossy. Mother expected all of us to make polite chitchat at mealtimes. All of us, that is, except for Granddaddy. He was allowed to stare into space and think deep thoughts, his mind adrift above the noise of our crowded table.

As usual, Travis sat next to me. I whispered, "Dr. Pritzker is going to make us something to keep the goats quiet."

"Really? That's a great idea."

Mother said, "There shall be no whispering at the table. Do you two have some item of conversation you'd like to share with the rest of us? Hmm?"

"Uh, no, Mother," I said. "Sorry."

Lamar smirked across the table at me. Why did he have to be that way? And why did I have to have *six* brothers? It was beyond unfair. If it had been up to me, I'd have kept Travis for sure and sent most of the others back.

I tried not to look like I was bolting my breakfast, but Mother noticed anyway. "Calpurnia," she said, "you are eating in a most unseemly manner."

This earned me another smirk from Lamar. I threw him my best fierce look in return. "Mother," I said, "may I please be excused?"

"You may." She gave me an odd look as I pushed away from the table, but then I'm used to her odd looks, I get so many of them. Once out of her sight, I broke into a run and didn't stop until I got to Dr. Pritzker's office.

"There you are, Calpurnia," he said, as I burst through his door. "Here's the stuff you need."

He handed me a small brown bottle with a cork in it. "I have to warn you, I've prepared this for horses and cattle before but never for goats."

"What is it, Dr. Pritzker?"

"It is a sedative mixture of root of aconite and powdered opium. I've tried to make the dose so that the animals are drowsy but not fast asleep. Mix it into a mash of oats and hot water an hour before the pageant. That should do the trick."

"Thank you, Dr. Pritzker; what do I owe you?"

He would never take my money, but

I still felt I had to ask. "There's no charge, Calpurnia."

"I'll wash bottles and make labels for you all next week."

"That would be much appreciated." I ran home clutching the bottle, thumb firmly on the cork.

6

The day before Christmas dawned chilly and overcast. Travis and I stirred up a mash and added Dr. Pritzker's medicine. I thought perhaps the goats might smell the medicine and refuse to eat it but, as usual, they gobbled up their food and looked around for more.

I kept a close eye on them while Travis and Harry hitched Arthur to the wagon. "Well," I said, "here we go. If this doesn't work, I don't know what we'll do."

Buster and Hattie dozed quietly as I entered their pen, the collars hidden behind my back. And you know what happened when I slipped them over their heads? Absolutely nothing. Buster licked my hand; Hattie snored softly.

We loaded the limp goats and my brothers into the wagon, and Harry drove us to church.

Reverend Barker was directing some

workmen who were putting the finishing touches on the shed and nailing the shiny star to the roof. They shifted bales of hay into position for Joseph and Mary and the shepherds to perch on. A cow and horse stood toward the back. The scene looked very nice (although it would have looked a whole lot nicer with a camel).

We gently set the goats in the straw, their eyelids drooping.

"So far, so good," I said to Travis. "I'll stay here while you put on your robes."

He went inside the church to get

ready. I kept watch over Buster and Hattie, but I needn't have bothered. They were busy falling fast asleep.

Granddaddy and Dr. Pritzker strolled by and stopped to chat.

"The goats are behaving, I see," said Dr. Pritzker. He turned to Granddaddy and told him about the sedative.

"Ah," said Granddaddy, "these goats have supped on the essence of opium

poppies from the Hindu Kush, where their ancestors once roamed."

"What's the Hindu Kush?" I said.

"A mountain range on the far side of the world. It's also the place where the ancestors of these goats evolved. We will look for it on the globe after dinner."

They wandered off, discussing the medicinal uses of various plants around the world.

Travis and the others came out in their robes and stood around the baby Jesus doll nestled in the straw. The three kings took their places. My friend Lula played an angel, and she looked really pretty with her golden halo and long hair spilling down her back.

"Hi, Lula," I said. "You look really nice."

"Thanks. I'm sorry you didn't get picked to play anyone this year."

"That's okay," I said. "I've been helping Travis with the animals."

At exactly two o'clock, the choir came out of the church. They stood off to one side and sang "Silent Night."

Reverend Barker read from the Bible: "'And she brought forth her firstborn son, and wrapped him in swaddling clothes, and laid him in a

manger, because there was no room for them in the inn.'"

To my relief, my brother and the animals stayed quiet. Just like the song said, all was calm, all was bright.

"'And shepherds were keeping watch over their flock by night.'" Travis kept watch over his flock of two, dozing peacefully in the straw.

I wished I could have caught up with Granddaddy and Dr. Pritzker and heard more about exotic plants and animals, but I'd promised Travis I'd stick around for a bit.

By the time three o'clock rolled

around, my stomach was grumbling for a snack. It occurred to me that Viola was probably taking her afternoon nap in between cooking lunch and dinner. This meant the cookie jar was likely to be unguarded—and full—unless that pill Lamar had swooped in earlier. I sidled up to Travis and whispered, "Everything's okay here. I'm going home to snag us some cookies. But I'll be right back."

"All right, Callie."

I was turning to leave when out of the corner of my eye I saw movement. I stopped in my tracks and turned. Oh no. It couldn't be. Buster was twitching.

He looked like he was straining mighty hard to open his eyes. He finally succeeded and looked around with a glassy gaze. He shuddered, took a few deep breaths, and hauled himself halfway up. And then Hattie's eyes flicked open. Uh-oh. Slowly . . . slowly . . . the goats were coming alive.

Travis whispered, "They're waking up, Callie. What do I do?"

"Don't panic," I said. "All you have to do is hold on to them. There's only an hour to go." (Even as the words came out of my mouth, it struck me how strange time can be. Have you ever

thought about how time can go fast or slow, depending? Think about it: Time at a birthday party goes by too fast; time practicing the piano goes by too slow. And time wrestling an unhappy goat goes on forever.)

Hattie struggled to her feet. "Travis," I hissed, "hold tight."

Then Buster struggled to *his* feet. They both stood there looking groggy. Travis clutched their flimsy leashes of twine. Hattie shook herself and fell sideways with a *whomp*. Joseph and Mary looked up in surprise. The other animals stirred.

"Hold her down," I said. "Keep her down." Lamar shushed us.

Hattie wobbled to her feet again, reached a hind foot forward, and scratched at her collar.

Buster *maa*-ed softly. Then a little louder. And then louder still. He grabbed a mouthful of straw. Hattie snatched a wisp from him and bolted it down. By now Buster was making a surprising amount of noise. Travis looked tense. The other actors turned to stare at him. The cow swished her tail; the horse stomped his foot.

"It's okay, Travis," I said. "Don't let go, whatever you do."

Buster stretched his neck toward the baby Jesus. He strained harder and harder, choking on his collar. Then—naturally—the twine snapped. He leaped forward and started eating the straw in the doll's bed. Not to be outdone, Hattie snapped her leash and followed suit.

"Noooo!" Travis yelled, and threw himself at them. He got his arms around Buster, who panicked and butted him in the face.

"Ow!" Travis let go and rubbed at

the red mark on his forehead. Hattie
chewed the hem of Travis's robe.

"Hey!" He pushed her away and fell
backward in the straw tangled up in his
robes, thrashing around like an upside-
down beetle.

"Help!"

"Travis," I said. "Calm down. Be

still." Buster stepped on him.

"Help me!"

This frightened Buster, which frightened Hattie, which frightened the cow, which frightened the horse. The cow mooed loudly and the horse reared up. The cow broke loose and ran away down the road; the horse broke

free and ran after her. The choir stampeded in all directions, their robes flapping like bats' wings.

"Wait," shouted Reverend Barker, "where are you going?"

Hattie decided that if the straw the rubber doll was lying in tasted good, the doll itself must taste even better. She stood up on her hind legs and munched on the toes. (It's funny how in the middle of a terrible mess, the strangest thoughts will pop into your head. What popped into mine at that moment was, *Huh, that's strange. Why would a goat eat a doll's toes? I bet they don't taste very good. But she looks like she's enjoying them. It's too bad we couldn't get a camel; it probably wouldn't be as bad-mannered as this. Followed by, Calpurnia, what are you doing? For goodness' sake, get a grip.*)

I hauled Travis to his feet. "You grab Buster," I said. "I'll grab Hattie. Come on, we have to get them out of here."

Travis tackled Buster and got his arms around the goat's neck, which should have worked, except that at that very second up ran a stray dog barking its head off. Buster yanked himself free from Travis and turned to face this new threat, lowering his head to show his horns. The dog, no doubt thinking it should be in charge, accepted the challenge and barked even louder. The terrible noise made it really hard to think. I shouted at the dog, "Stop it!" but of course the dog did not stop it.

I grabbed Hattie, and she kicked me in the shins—oh boy, did that hurt—but I managed to hold on. There would be time enough for rubbing sore shins later. Right now we had a panic on our hands.

Lamar yelled at me and Travis, "What are you doing? You're messing it all up."

Oh, right, like it was all *our* fault. The unfairness of it made me want to punch him, and I would have if he'd been within punching range. But he wasn't, and I didn't have to. Buster did it for me. The goat ran at my brother and butted him off his feet. He flew through the air and landed against one of the poles supporting the roof with a loud *craaackk.*

The shock on my brother's face was so perfect, so wonderful, it was the best Christmas gift ever. I would treasure it my whole life.

From overhead, we heard a steady

creaking growing louder. We looked up
at the roof, which, oddly, seemed to be
tilting. Yep, definitely moving. No
more time for gloating.

Reverend Barker yelled, "Get out,
get out, get out!" He rolled Lamar out
of the way and dragged Lula behind
him.

The creaking got louder and louder.

Travis and I scrambled backward,
still holding the goats, and made it to
the street.

We turned and watched as the shed
tipped sideways. And . . . slowly . . .
slowly . . . fell down.

7

The good news is that no one was hurt very badly. My shins were sore for a couple of days from Hattie, and Travis had a mark on his forehead from Buster that soon faded. The one that took the longest to heal was that pill Lamar. Oh, not because he was physically hurt, but because Buster had so sorely abused his dignity. I figured it served him right.

Our Christmas was rather quiet that year. My father gave money to build a new shed. Travis was banned from the pageant for life, which we both thought a bit unfair. Oh, and goats were banned from all future pageants as well, which everyone agreed was a perfectly sensible decision.

Hattie and Buster, no worse for the wear, were safely returned to Mr. Morgan, who praised their condition.

"Well," he said, "I can tell you've

done a fine job looking after them. It seems you have a knack for this. Maybe you'd like to keep these two and raise them as your own. What do you think about that?"

I looked sideways at Travis, expecting him to jump at this offer. In which case I'd have smacked him, truly. But for once in his life, the boy was silent. What a relief. We ended up taking home no goats.

To those of you reading this, I hope you've learned this lesson: The main trouble with goats is that they'll eat just about anything.